DEDICATION

To:

Alaysia, Donald III, Skilar, Jayden, Isaiah, Zoe, Erza, Britain & Jade.

Always Listen to your parents and know who you are.....

Love always,
Uncle Shaad.

THE ADVENTURES OF PRINCE ISAIAH

Once upon a time there was a magical Kingdom called,
Timbuktu. The leaders of this kingdom were King Yanis
and Queen Azella. They had 2 children; a boy, named
Prince Isaiah and a girl, named Princess Ameena.

Everyone in the Kingdom was happy. The people loved the Royal Family because the King and Queen always made sure everyone had food to eat. Prince Isaiah even opened his own fruit and vegetables stand to make sure everyone had healthy food choices.

...But one week, the King had to travel to a meeting and that's when the wicked dragon from the east came and stole all the food.

Prince Isaiah ran back home and told the Queen. "Mother, mother, the dragon has taken all of our food and he flew to the mountains. What are we going to do?"

"Calm down son, we will take care of that dragon. For now just take this bucket and go down to the river and get some water. Since the dragon has taken most of the food, we will have to prepare soup for the Kingdom."

Isaiah listened to his mother and went to get water. When he got to the lake, he could not believe what he saw.

The dragon was drinking all the water!

Isaiah screamed, "Hey, you mean dragon, we need that water for our Kingdom. We can only make soup since you took all of our food."

The dragon looked at Prince Isaiah and said, "Oh, don't worry, young Prince, I think it will rain today. You can get your soup from the sky. Haha Haha!"

The dragon flew away and Isaiah was forced to walk home with no water. As he was walking home, he noticed something sticking out of the ground, it was a vase.

He walked over to it, he picked it up....

....(BOOM! BANG!!!)

There was a loud explosion and smoke was coming from the vase.

"Argggghhh, who has disturbed me out of my sleep?," said the voice.

"Who are you?" said Prince Isaiah

A voice came from the vase and said, "I am Genie... and whoever touches this vase, I have to grant them 2 wishes. Ask for anything and your wish is my command."

"So let me get this right...", said Prince Isaiah. "You are saying that I can ask for anything and you will give it to me?"

"Yes", said Genie.

Isaiah thought to himself, and he then yelled, "Please give me a hero to defeat the red dragon!"

Genie closed his eyes and then...

(BOOM! BANG!!!)

There was a loud noise and smoke everywhere. Then a man appeared.

He was big and strong and he was dressed in shiny medals.

"Who are you", asked Prince Isaiah. The man spoke in a very deep and powerful voice, "I am the Honorable Marcus Mosiah Garvey. How can I help you?"

Isaiah said, "Mr. Garvey, the wicked red dragon is taking all of our food. See, there he is now."

Isaiah pointed to the dragon

"Oh no," said Isaiah.

"What is it," asked Marcus Garvey.

The Prince looked very worried as he begins to speak, "I think the dragon is headed for the food storage. That's the only food we have left!"

They ran back to the Castle to check on the food storage, but when they got there, they found that the dragon had broken through the wall

They walked inside and sure enough the dragon was in there, eating all the food.

(Yum yum yum yum yum yum)

"Dragon, You ate everything!," said Isaiah.

"Almost everything!," said the dragon.
The dragon pulled out a jar of red sauce.

"What is this? Cherry jam? Or maybe strawberry jelly?" asked the dragon.

Isaiah said, "No, it's fire pepper sauce."

"What?" said the dragon.

"Nothing!," yelled Garvey! "Eat up dragon, just make sure you save us a little!"

"Haha haha, you wish," said the dragon. "This is all mine!" (Yum yum yum yum!)

Then the dragon's eyes begin to water, he tried to open his mouth to speak, but as soon as he did, a great big ball of fire came flying out of his mouth....

"*AHHHHHHHHHHH!* This is not strawberry jelly," wheezed the dragon.

"No," said Isaiah, "It... was Fire Peppers from the South Mountains, the hottest in the land."

"Water! Give me water!," said the dragon.

Isaiah smiled and said, "You drank all the water, don't you remember?"

Marcus Garvey rolled up his sleeves, his muscles began to get bigger and bigger.

"You want some water dragon? There's some at the ocean," said Marcus Garvey.

"The ocean is a 2 weeks journey from here...," said the dragon.

"Exactly," said Marcus Garvey, "You don't have much time to waste."

He grabbed the dragon by his tail and his neck.

"What are you doing?" said the dragon.

"Well, the way I figure, if you need water now, and the ocean is a 2 week journey away, I have to get you there fast."

Marcus Garvey took the dragon outside and stretched him as far as he could.

The dragon yelled, "Hold on, wait, I don't know if I'm ready..."

Marcus Garvey chuckled, "Oh, you look ready to me. What do you think Prince Isaiah? Does he look ready to you?"

"He looks ready to me," said Prince Isaiah.

Marcus Garvey stretched and stretched and stretched the dragon as far he could...and then SNAP, he let him go!

The dragon flew away into the air until the point where they could no longer see him. The dragon was gone forever.

Isaiah looked at Marcus Garvey, "Thank you, Mr. Garvey, thank you! I would not have defeated the dragon without you."

"We did it together young prince and team work makes the dream work.
I must be going now, but I will always be around if you need me."

Marcus Garvey shook Prince Isaiah's hand and he disappeared.

Then suddenly, Isaiah remembered he had one more wish. "Genie, I still have one more wish right?"

"Yes prince," mumbled Genie.

Isaiah said, "Well then, I wish you to be free from this vase and free to live your life!"

(BOOM! BANG!!!)

There was a loud thunderous noise and smoke everywhere. It was done. Finally, after spending thousands of years trapped, Genie was free from the vase.

Genie yelled, "Thank you Prince Isaiah, thank you!"

Prince Isaiah replied, "You are welcome my friend. We all deserve to be free."

And everyone lived happily ever after. The End.

"LIBERATE THE MINDS OF MEN
AND ULTIMATELY YOU WILL
LIBERATE THE BODIES OF MEN"

MARCUS GARVEY

Made in the USA
Monee, IL
17 August 2023